D1527763

The Sleepers of Roraima

by the same author

*

TUMATUMARI
THE WAITING ROOM
THE EYE OF THE SCARECROW
HEARTLAND
THE WHOLE ARMOUR
THE FAR JOURNEY OF OUDIN
PALACE OF THE PEACOCK
ASCENT TO OMAI

The Sleepers of Roraima

A CARIB TRILOGY

Wilson Harris

With drawings by
Karen Usborne

FABER AND FABER
London

First published in 1970
by Faber and Faber Limited
24 Russell Square London WC1
Printed in Great Britain by
Latimer Trend & Co Ltd Plymouth
All rights reserved

ISBN 0 571 09272 1

for Margaret
Alexis and Denise

Contents

Author's Note

Roraima (setting of Conan Doyle's *Lost World*) is said to possess the highest mural rock face in the world. It looks towards Brazil, Guiana and Venezuela and one of its Carib names is the 'Night Mountain' since it is often enveloped in a blanket of cloud.

NOTE

The Caribs have virtually disappeared as a people though their name is attached to the islands of the Caribbean sea and remnants of their mythology can be traced deep into the South American continent.

This story is an invention based on one of their little-known myths— the myth of couvade.

The purpose of couvade *was to hand on the legacy of the tribe— courage and fasting—to every newborn child. All ancestors were involved in this dream—animal as well as human, bird as well as fish. The dust of every thing, cassava bread (the Caribs' staple diet), the paint of war, the cave of memories, were turned into a fable of history—the dream of* couvade.

Couvade

"The name you bear," the old Carib said to Couvade his grand-son, "means *sleeper of the tribe*."

"Why did you give me this name?" Couvade asked.

"Because of your parents. . . ."

"But I do not know my parents."

"Ah," the old man sighed.

"And anyhow what have they got to do with my name?"

"They broke a certain rule." His grandfather's face wrinkled and darkened like a reflection in the river at their doorstep.

"I don't understand. What rule did they break?"

"An old rule. Few abide by it now. We are a dying tribe. A shadow of what we once were." He looked shaken and tired.

"Tell me, grandfather," Couvade insisted. "I'm old enough to be told. After all I am ten years now." His eyes grew a little defiant since he knew there was no record of the day he was born, the month or year, except by word of mouth.

Couvade's hair was black as the river. Thick on his head and glistening in the candlelight of the hut. The old man stroked it gently. In the half-shadow above his grandson's glistening head it was as if he were intent on immersing himself in a river of reflection which ran through him into this uncertain child of the future. He shivered a little thinking how reduced in numbers his people were. They had been almost wiped out over the

centuries through foreign invasion as well as inter-tribal con-
flict. He shivered again. It was cold at night this time of the
year. Starred sky. Thick dew. Inky forest.

"Tell me," Couvade said again.

"You were born on a night like this," his grandfather began.
"Your mother and father fell sick. . . ." He stopped.

"Please go on, grandfather," Couvade urged. "I do so want
to know the secret of my name."

The old man looked away from the boy into the far distance
and spoke as if to himself. "They fell sick—it was the sickness
of the soul."

"I do not understand. . . ."

His grandfather looked back at him speaking in a strange
quiet voice. "It is a dream. A dream of hunter and hunted. You
will find it recorded—this dream—on the rocks and in the caves.
Hunter and hunted."

"What did they dream?"

"They dreamed—they dreamed the forest grew black as a
cave and the stars were extinguished. All they could hear was
the sound of wings multiplied like the thunder of a waterfall."

He stopped. But Couvade continued to listen to the ancestral
voices of waterfall and forest. He knew of the guacharo bird—
how its uncanny reflexes (piercing vision and echoing wings)
guided it through the darkest underground caves. It lived deep
in the earth where there wasn't a sprinkle of light. Never flew
abroad until dark. Carried a star under its wings which the
Indians called the "night's eye" and from which they made
their candles—large wax-like bait on a hook suspended from
the roof.

Grandfather and grandson now sat—two of the last surviving
members of the fishermen of night (as their ancient tribe was
called)—under the flickering bait of the candle-light in the
room.

"I want to know more of my parents," Couvade cried. "Where did they go? What happened to them?"

The old man sighed again. "When you were born and your parents fell ill," he said, "there was only one remedy for their kind of sickness—the ancient remedy of *couvade*. This meant seclusion—a season of fasting and seclusion. They had to shut themselves away from the outside world. No speech with the tribe who would undertake to provide them with vegetables or fruit by leaving it, at the end of each day, at the door of their hut which stood at the end of the village. *No meat or fish*. This was strictly forbidden."

"But they ate. . . ?" Couvade asked with a sudden sense of foreboding.

The old man appeared very tired as if the sap of life within him were declining. He touched his grandson like one who wished to gain strength from his young limbs and to confer at the same time a trickle of wisdom. "They broke the law of *couvade*," he said at last. "They ate what had been forbidden. That very night we were attacked by the huntsmen of night—the tribe to the west of us—and your parents . . . they were never seen again."

"They were taken prisoner?" Couvade asked breathlessly.

"I cannot tell what happened," the old man said sadly, "I only know they broke the dream of *couvade*." His voice trembled. "It was I who found you, an infant six weeks old, at the entrance of a cave just outside the village where they hid you from the wild huntsmen. I believe they fled into the forest." He shook his head. "I do not know. Perhaps they were indeed taken prisoner."

His voice died away in a dry whisper and the old man and the boy sat, each wrapped in his own blanket of memory and questioning. All was still save for the cry of a bird in the forest asking over and over in plaintive tones, "Who you? Who you?"

2

Later, asleep in his hammock, Couvade dreamt that he had returned to the cave where his parents had hidden him in the nightmare flight from the huntsmen of night. It was as if in his dream he was beginning to understand something of the secret of his name—that he was part of some strange dream of history in which his grandfather's people feared they would vanish from the face of the earth.

The walls of the cave were painted with many curious creatures. Birds. Fish. Men and women who were half-bird, half-fish. Scenes of the hunt. There were two figures in particular that fascinated him and they seemed to be coming alive on the wall of the cave. A man and a woman dressed as curious birds. Perhaps some strange owl or guacharo bird since they wore sunglasses—American sunglasses (in the ridiculous way of dreams) Couvade had seen fall from the sky in the wake of a passing aeroplane. Though they were actually coming alive on the wall of the cave and Couvade felt that all he had to do was reach out and touch them, he had the sensation that they were still far removed from him. Divided from him by water, light, and by other elements. By war: news had trickled through to the last members of the tribe that the great world beyond the great forest, beyond the Carib sea, was at war. It had all happened within the ten years since he was born.

First of all there was water and Couvade decided to swim across to them—the figures coming alive on the wall of ancestors. He would change himself into a fish like one of the paintings there. Half-boy, half-fish. On the other hand if he changed into a bird—half-boy, half-bird—he could fly across the river and approach the two bird-like figures—listen to their conversation. They would accept him as something or someone they need not worry about, not realising, of course, that he was a spy. So—in his dream—he made up his mind. There was a feathered head-dress on the ground which he placed over his hair and wings which he stuck to his sides. A pair of sunglasses also which gave him the sense of belonging to the twentieth century while giving him a secretive look as well—an entombed piercing look as if he came from the remote past.

Now that he was ready he began to fly across the dividing river of the cave towards the strangers on the wall. But he felt himself beaten back by a wind of fear. He decided he would never make it in this way and his best plan would be to do what he had first thought of—turn himself into a fish and swim. So Couvade undressed again, took off his glasses, feathered head-dress and wings and clad himself now in fish's scales and eyes.

He slipped into the water and began to swim towards the masked strangers on the wall. He had reached about half-way when he was beaten back again by the water of fear. And in his dream this fear was very strong.

He so much wanted to reach the live figures on the other side of the river of the cave who seemed to him strangers painted there and yet at the same time familiars of flesh and blood. *His flesh and blood. Could they truly be his lost parents after all?* He had now tried wearing two disguises—half-bird, half-fish—in order to reach them but nothing had worked. Nothing had taken him *there*. He had wanted to deceive them so that they wouldn't think him an intruder in their midst. . . . He began to wonder—was it necessary to creep up on them unawares and try to deceive them, if they were really his parents?

Perhaps this was where he had made his mistake. He must go across to them just as he was. No disguises, no tricks.

He carefully restored the head-dress, spectacles, feathers to the ground of the cave, the scales and eyes of the fish to the wall where they shone now like stars and constellations. He approached the river to let himself in again but as he was about to do so he was startled by his own reflection. There were faint ripples in the stream which suddenly seemed to give him an entirely wrinkled old expression. He shrank away from the water as if he had been beaten back this time by the *wrinkles* of fear. It was foolish but there it was.

He began to have a glimmering understanding of what was happening to him. In his sleep he had entered the cave of ancestors and was learning to see himself with the eyes of night. The cave of ancestors where nothing was new under the sun and yet where everything was masked and strange.

The cave was very old—old as the womb—old as the guacharo bird: it was very young—young as space—young as an aeroplane whose sunglasses falling from the sky belonged to his own masked parents. Masked curious birds. *They were searching for him, Couvade felt, as he was searching for them.* Lost tribes. Lost parents. Lost child.

Couvade decided that he must look for a bridge to cross to them. Perhaps if he coated himself, powdered himself with earth, his parents on the other side would recognize him as someone who had travelled great distances to meet them and so naturally was as travel-stained as they. They might take pity on him if they saw him in such a guise. So he began to scrape the floor of the cave until he accumulated a small heap of dust, white as cassava bread. This he sprinkled carefully on his brow and hair, arms and legs until he felt he looked travel-stained and weary.

He returned to the river in the middle of the cave and this time he could see himself in the wrinkled water like a branch, all covered with ragged blossom. So ragged that when he shook himself lightly the long accumulated dust of the cave began to descend towards the river like mist. A faint bridge—

misty, dusty—stretched now across the river of souls and Couvade set out towards his parents on the opposite side of the cave. He was half-way across when the mist grew so thick he could barely see the back of his hand. He turned and looked back. NOTHING. He turned and looked forward. NOTHING. Yet the bridge stood solid—ages and ages on either side. A bridge which was so travel-stained it might have been formed by the mists of time. Pursuers and pursued. Hunter and hunted. Couvade was uncertain now which end of the bridge he had started from.

He proceeded very slowly and with great caution toward where he judged his parents to be. At long last the mist began to clear a little and he came upon the other bank of the stream. *Yes*—he felt convinced now—he had succeeded in crossing the bridge of souls. But—to his sadness—the two parent figures were no longer there. Instead a great forest reached down to the edge of the water: green-heart trees looking faintly silvery and golden. He remembered his grandfather had spoken of this land on the other side of the cave: the forest of the huntsmen of night. No one was there to greet him but he saw that they had left their sunglasses suspended from a branch. Their head-dress too and the scales and eyes of a fish like a starry cloak which shone in the water against the trees. Couvade was glad. It was as if they wished to surrender to him all their disguises as he had surrendered his to them on his side of the cave.

The trail into the forest followed the river and he set out along this. He had walked about a hundred yards when he came upon a hill of dust: hill of cassava bread: it resembled the one he had scraped together on the floor of the cave to sprinkle himself with and build his bridge. He poked at it with a finger and a wrinkled face peered out at the heart of the hill, which reminded him of his own reflection in the river not long ago save that this face did not beat him back with a look of fear. It was friendly—an ancient grinning lizard. It changed its colours as it moved—sometimes pale, sometimes dark, sometimes silver, sometimes gold like the hill on which it moved. Silver cassava bread, golden cassava bread.

"You're travel-stained," Couvade said, "like my bridge of souls. I can see that."

"Travel-stained as the rainbow," the lizard smiled.

"I'm looking for my parents," Couvade said.

"I'll see what I can do," the lizard said. "Follow me."

So, still in his dream, Couvade followed the lizard as it moved along the wall of the forest. It kept changing colours all the way—sometimes it looked like a star or a fish, sometimes like a feather or a leaf. It was as if the colours it created were a bridge—an endless bridge spanning all the tribes, all the masks of ancestors. Couvade smiled at the lizard. As he smiled he seemed to wake . . . Broad daylight . . . The wizened face of his grandfather stood above him and the wizened hands of his grandfather were shaking his hammock.

3

Couvade had dreamt that he awoke but in truth the wizened face and wizened hands were all still part and parcel of a dream painted on the wall of ancestors. It was so real, however, that it was all coming alive. The tiny village where they lived—painted on the wall of Couvade's dream—stood on its last legs in broad daylight in the night of history. Couvade and his grandfather were amongst the last surviving members of an old Carib tribe who prolonged an ancient feud with the huntsmen of night. The old man said to Couvade in the dream—"Wake up. Wake up Couvade. It's time to move on. Our enemies are after us."

Couvade sprang up and they began to pack their few belongings. First of all the sunglasses which had descended one day from the sky over the jungle in the wake of a passing aeroplane. Next—the head-dress of feathers, a relic of the past belonging to the old man's vanished son (Couvade's father). Then—scales and eyes of a fish—a kind of dancer's cloak—belonging to the vanished woman his mother.

"Why must we leave this place grandfather?" Couvade asked.

"I fear our enemies," the old man said. "They were seen by the cave beyond our village during the night. Skulking against the wall. Those bird-people are no parents of yours. No relatives of any kind. Looking like animated skeletons. Nothing but a trick to take us in—believe me Couvade. We must hide. Conceal ourselves." He pointed to a lizard on the roof. "See," he said. "It has acquired the colour of a dry leaf. It looks like dust. We too must fly like dust in the wind. It is the only way. We must fly—I tell you."

And so they set out—grandfather and grandson and the nightmare relic of the ancient tribe—across the bridge of deceptions—the bridge of dreams painted on the wall of their cave.

They arrived first at the Bush known as the Bush of the Toucan. It stood on the bank of the river and the old man placed the feathered dress that had once been his son's upon Couvade's head. He sprinkled it with dust and said—"This was where my son (your father) stood at the Battle of the Toucan. In those days our enemies were the fishermen of night."

"But . . . but . . ." Couvade could not help stammering a little "that is impossible . . . we are the fishermen of night and our enemies the huntsmen of night. . . . Perhaps you are so old grandfather that you forget our real name."

"We called ourselves feathers of the toucan long long ago,"

the old man said, "before we became fishermen of night and our enemies (the fishermen of night) became huntsmen of night."

He again sprinkled—with a cunning smile—the dust of the Place of the Toucan upon his grandson's head. It was like a curious initiation into the secret of names and Couvade recalled the river of reflection and the hill of dust, gold and silver masks of the lizard. It was now daylight in his dream but under the trees against the river, in the very heart of the forest, he felt he stood still upon the travel-stained bridge of the tribes wondering which way to go: dusty feathers of the toucan, misty fishermen of night, black huntsmen of night. They were one and the same—the cruel tricks and divisions of mankind, the cruel ruses and battles of mankind. He remembered the strange bird-like figures he had seen across the river who appeared to be both enemy and friend: he had accepted them as his lost parents, but his grandfather had seen them as animated skeletons, the clever and treacherous disguises the enemy wore —huntsmen of night. He (Couvade) had tried to fly *to* them, swim to them, cross to them, travel-stain himself, dress and undress himself to meet them, whereas his grandfather wished to fly *from* them, run from them, hide from them—hide *in* them (as a last resort) in their cloak, in their name.

"Time to go," said the old man looking back over his shoulder as if he feared his pursuers and looking forward over his grandson's head as if he saw someone flitting before him in Couvade's dream. Hunter and hunted. Could they be one and the same in the end?

"Time to go," he repeated.

"But why can't we rest here?" said Couvade. "I'm very tired."

"Impossible," said the wrinkled lizard face of his grandfather. "We must change our address. Change our colour. We must move on."

So Couvade was persuaded to take the trail again across the Bridge of Ruses—Bridge of the Trickster—Bridge of Tribes. Deeper and deeper into the forest with the river running at their side—sometimes smooth as an infant's brow, sometimes littered with boulders in a waterfall.

"We still have a little way to go to reach the Place of the Fish. It was there long ago that we changed our name: rubbed ourselves all over with the grease of the candle—bait of light— fishermen of night. No longer did we dance by the sun of the toucan but with the shadow of night. . . ." His grandfather paused.

Couvade sighed. Were he and his grandfather running from and towards the same darkness, the same light, the same dance, the same stillness? All these years and still they ran around in a great circle—feathers of the toucan, candle of the guacharo, fishermen of night, huntsmen of night—always one step away from the centre of peace the end of war.

They paused for a while on the bank of the river to take stock of the Bridge of Masks painted on the wall of dreams. Couvade climbed on the shoulders of a rock. This provided him with a view along the stream towards the Place of the Toucan. It was all very strange because it seemed to lie behind them but yet seemed equally to lie in the mists ahead. A frail rainbow lay across an ancient battleground of memory. Like feathers of cloud. Peacock flag as well as toucan, parrot as well as macaw. Green and red and blue, yellow and white—shade upon shade, shade within shade. It was so exquisite and beautiful Couvade wondered why they had ever left it and whether one day they would retrace their steps into the light of the sun. Whether, in fact, it lay genuinely behind or before them now—at this end of his bridge or that—the rainbow of mankind.

"It's no use," his grandfather said as if he had read his thoughts. "Whether backwards or forwards we must go on to the Place of the Fish. It's less spectacular than the Toucan. It's where we started from when we became fishermen. It's still our only chance." He looked back over his shoulder with the air of a man frightened of both substance and shadow, past and future.

They set out again towards the Place of the Fish. The trees of the forest sometimes shone with flame. First they came to a red tree—a kind of cedar or glowing purpleheart. On one of its branches a beam of sun dangled like a feather, a tuft of feathers, a bright orchid. Shone with such brilliance Couvade thought of a glory of birds, rainbow of the tribes. It was as if as the small party—the last of the ancient tribe—made its way along the Bridge of Souls, one could perceive the trail of the toucan like a strange lizard, a feathery lizard, that absorbed the dying colours of the sun.

Second they came upon a bright-green snake, the parrot snake. It darted on the path before them like a messenger of the elements. Again it seemed like a chain of feathers born of the sun which had pierced the primeval forest in a glancing path upon the Bridge of Tribes.

"Feathers of the Toucan," said his grandfather. "The ghosts of the past. They will lead us to the Place of the Fish."

The trail, in fact, was marked by these witnesses, the feathers of the sun. After the green snake they came upon a russet branch—a bonfire of leaves—burning blossom. Each leaf or feather shone with transparency like the powder of space. One by one, tuft by tuft, each feather of the toucan danced before them. Led them forward upon the trail towards the Place of the Fish.

They arrived at the Place of the Fish towards nightfall. It was an open clearing near the river bank and in some ways not unlike their other stopping places. In the setting sun—as the feathers of the toucan vanished—the old man placed the scales and eyes of the fish upon Couvade's head. Initiation into the motherhood of the tribe: origins of the fishermen of night. Couvade's mother had been a dancer of the fish.

Couvade gave a cry of joy and pointed to the wall of the sky. Lit up as if for her (his mother's) dance. He remembered the hill of dust which had been sprinkled on his head and which now gleamed afresh like shooting stars. Stars. The largest and brightest he had ever seen. Surely all he had to do was shake himself lightly—as lightly as before when he built his bridge of souls—so lightly that the dust on his head would scatter into a shining net, the brightest, most shining net in all the world. Fishermen of night. Net of stars.

He shook himself now—the dust of stars—as if he too danced to the music of the river. In fact his feet began to move and spin. Ballet of the fish. Dance of the fish. Song of the river. Net of the river. He said to his grandfather in an ecstasy of happiness, "I have caught her. My mother. She sings and dances in my net, in my heart. Song and dance of the fish painted on the wall of the cave."

But his grandfather cried "hush! it's a trick to make you sleep, then the enemy will take you away, make you her prisoner. *Their* prisoner. Believe me, Couvade, I tell you truly."

Couvade only laughed merrily as if the laughter of the fish made his heart light as a feather. "But I already sleep" he said. "Have you forgotten grandfather I am the sleeper of the tribe upon the bridge of dreams? What harm can it do to sleep . . .?" Couvade laughed gaily at the riddle of the night.

But his grandfather cried "there is sleep and sleep. Sleep of enemy and sleep of friend." He wrenched the net from Couvade's hand telling him it was another trick of the enemy, the cunning enemy.

Couvade gave a loud cry. The net which had been torn from his hands settled into the river of night and sank to the bottom of the painted cave. The song of the fish ceased. The dance of the fish was over. He sat now subdued and silent under the shadow of the cold stars.

The small party huddled together (a group of shadowy figures) not daring to light a fire. They munched cassava—dry cakes which dissolved into powder. As the night advanced the cold stars continued to shine on their lips with the dust of bread and the eyes of silent fish, no longer darting and dancing on their painted wall of dreams. The old man was sad. Sad that he had rebuked Couvade. But he had had no alternative. This was Couvade's initiation into the recurring motherhood of the tribe and the recurring death of the tribe, recurring song of the tribe, recurring silence of the tribe. "Soon we shall cease to be fishermen of night," he said sorrowfully to his grandson, "it is time to go."

But Couvade felt miserable and obstinate. He longed to hold again the shining net and hear the music of the river. "I thought you said it would be safe here grandfather," he complained, "I am sure that was my mother I saw dancing—coming alive on the wall of the cave—on the bridge of tribes."

"It is never safe on the bridge of tribes," his grandfather told him, "what you saw were skulking enemies, animated skeletons. Your mother? No, I tell you. It was not she. It's another trick. They want to draw us out, make us dance foolishly, make a spectacle of ourselves."

"Shall we become huntsmen of night?" Couvade asked forlornly. "Shall we shed our skins and take the name of our enemies? Then perhaps we shall have come home at last." He spoke like someone repeating the lines of a sad play, a dream-play of history. He was so tired after their long journey. The figure he had been so sure was his mother had now turned into one of their pursuers and enemies according to his grand-father.

Long before dawn (when the night was still black about them) they set out again. First they came to a tree, or what Couvade thought must be a tree, in which the bird of night had settled. He touched the sleeping bird as if he had eyes in his fingers. He remembered the glowing trail of feathers they followed to the Place of the Fish. Now the feathers were inky, black as the trail of night. At the Place of the Fish he had felt he was in the presence of his mother and now, as he touched the sleeping bird, it seemed to him that he was in the presence of his father. His heart began to beat with excitement but before he could take a firm hold on its wings the bird of night started up and flew ahead of him. Its black feathers were displayed where the toucan's had been. It was the most cunning ruse to follow—the trail of the guacharo—the innermost secret of the lizard.

"My father," Couvade cried. "It is he. I felt him under my hands on the tree of night."

"No," his grandfather warned. "It was nothing. I told you before, I tell you again, it was just the night's change of face. Tricks of the enemy."

As the bird of night flew before them however, his impression of his lost father being found returned to Couvade strongly. He related it to the piercing vision of the bird of darkness: how it flew abroad at night within the cave of dreams and was able to penetrate the darkest places in search of food. As Couvade yearned towards it, it descended suddenly and brushed against his lips with a fall of fruit, cocerite of the forest. Couvade was sure his grandfather was wrong. This was no trick. He had touched it with his fingers a little while ago and now, in return, it touched him gently with its beak and wings. "My father" he breathed, so softly that his grandfather would not hear.

The members of the tribe stopped to consume the cocerite on the ground which the bird had given to them. And the bird too— draped in the darkness—stopped overhead, almost within his grasp Couvade felt. Nothing spectacular like the bridghead of the toucan, flame of the parrot, exotic head-dress of the sun, yet in its outline of memory it seemed to have settled at last, come home at last (his father in an intimate cloak, ancestral bird-cloak, knowing disguise in the wall of night). Couvade reached out with certainty and held it at last. He felt it respond to his grasp, secret and measureless, both creature and creation. As if his father danced too upon the wings of night—as his mother had danced within the net of night. And the feathers of his cloak were a sign of irrepressible humour and confidence. The gaiety of both his parents seemed in remarkable contrast to the sad fierce caution of his grandfather. And yet in some strange way their combined personalities, father, mother, grandfather, represented a royal strain in the tribe.

"My father," Couvade cried aloud as he held the bird-cloak, "my own father at last." But his grandfather cried in turn, "Your father is also my son. This is no son of mine." He tore the cloak from Couvade's grasp and the bird of night fluttered and flew ahead once more. Couvade gave a great sob: he felt nothing now save the shell of cocerite like a sharp quill in his hand. It pricked him with the black feather of night.

His grandfather said to him gently, "I warned you Couvade. Why won't you trust me?" He reached out and touched his arm and as he did so the dawn began to break. Couvade found that he possessed a misty view of the river, back to the Place of the Fish. In the same way—on his journey to the Place of the Fish —he had looked backwards or forwards to the Place of the Toucan. But whereas he had seen the Place of the Toucan arched by a rainbow, he now saw the Place of the Fish arched by a gigantic feather—a black feather, one of the last lingering feathers of the bird of night, the ancestral cloak of night, the *father* of night. In the pale light of dawn, Couvade saw too a dark trail of feathers which stretched from the Place of the Fish to where they now were in the forest. His attention however was riveted on the gigantic feather arched in the sky, upon which the luminous dawn was beginning to shine. As the light brightened the feather of the toucan (feather of day), feather of the guacharo (feather of night) began to dance over the Place of the Fish, the Place of the Fish which was no other than the Place of the Toucan.

The fish-net of his mother, which was no other than the bird-cloak of his father, whirled and danced in the sky, then settled itself into the bridge of dawn. Couvade felt the presence of both his lost parents crossing and re-crossing the shimmering bridge.

4

Couvade suddenly realized as the light broke in the cave—on the wall of dreams—that they had come around in a great circle. He said to his grandfather—"It's our old village grandfather. Village of the fisherman of night. Our old village. We've returned."

"No," said his grandfather shading his eyes against the rising bridge of the sun. "That village lies to the east of us. Yesterday it was to the west. It's the village of our enemies, the huntsmen of night. We shall hide here—in the mouth of this cave—until night falls. Then we shall enter and attack."

"It looks," said Couvade rubbing his eyes in turn as if he were just awakening from his dream—the dream of history, "it looks like our old village—our own village, the fishermen of night."

"It's the old village of our enemies Couvade. I remember it well. We shall descend on them—take their name, mask, colour. We shall become huntsmen of night. It's our safest hiding place.

That's why we've come all this way across the Bridge of Tribes."

"Do you mean this will be the last of the enemy? From now on we shall have no one to fear . . . ?"

"We shall wait until night falls. We shall enter. We shall attack."

"But there's no one there," cried Couvade. "The village is empty."

"Everyone is there," said the old man. "Keep your head down or they will see you. The village is full. Full of eyes and old memories. We shall take them by surprise."

During the day the old man laid his plans. Couvade was to remain within the mouth of the cave wrapped in a blanket— the ancient blanket of ancestors upon which the Bridge of Tribes had been stitched with the thread of the rainbow, the feathers of night, the Place of the Toucan, the Place of the Fish. Numerous other travel-stained threads—the threads of fate. The long endless thread and bridge of dreams upon which they followed the design of the enemy back to their own design and homestead—into their own design and hearth—into the design of parent and friend. For the hiding place of the enemy became their own secret like the secret of a friend. Their own home. Their own nest.

The old man himself—who would lead the attack—clad himself in the armour of the lizard. His companions—the remnant of the tribe whom he would lead—also clad themselves in the cloak of the lizard. In this way it was difficult to tell who was old and who young. This camouflage, in fact, was the major stratagem of attack which the old man had in mind. Three phases he explained to Couvade in the mouth of the cave. Three bridges which were the same painting on the wall of dreams.

First, in the light of the setting sun, when they could be observed by the enemy, they would enter the village across

THE BRIDGE OF THE AGED. So called because its withered planks looked like bones and skeletons.

On reaching the middle of the bridge they would pause for a while like icons or statues rather than living men. And gradually the chameleon cloak they wore (the armour of the lizard) would take on the colour of the bridge until they turned to sticks— ancient skeletons and sticks. The enemy would laugh as at an army of old men—beaten before the fight began. Thus they would cross their first bridge unmolested.

On the second bridge into the village the enemy would still perceive them (the old man calculated) by the setting sun. This bridge—coming after THE BRIDGE OF THE AGED— was known as THE BRIDGE OF THE CHILDREN. It resembled Couvade's blanket in its markings. Light as a hammock strung across a stream. So light it seemed the first puff of night would blow it away. The armour of the lizard on reaching THE BRIDGE OF THE CHILDREN would turn into wisps of cloth, wisps of thread, a tattered hammock or flag. The enemy would be consoled by *their* approaching enemy which was surely no enemy at all. Babes in the wood. Half-cradle, half-hearse of history. At one moment they looked decrepit and old, shrunken, almost non-existent, the next they looked threadbare, thin—a contemptible flag of souls.

COUVADE SUDDENLY HAD THE IMPRESSION HE HAD BEEN DREAMING ALL HIS LIFE WITHIN THE CAVE OF ANCESTORS AND THAT DREAM HAD BECOME BOTH THE BRIDGE OF THE AGED AND THE BRIDGE OF THE CHILDREN WOVEN UPON THE BLANKET TUCKED AROUND HIM. . . .

Thus far then the old man felt his plans had been well laid and he would safely outwit the enemy. But the third and last bridge —the most difficult of all—remained to be taken. This was THE BRIDGE OF NAMES he explained to Couvade. Here the enemy must finally be drawn and routed by the most secret ruse of the Lizard. For on THE BRIDGE OF NAMES in the pale shadow of the sun—the vanished sun—the armour of the lizard would take on the camouflage of *nothing*. . . .

5

The battle on THE BRIDGE OF NAMES began soon after nightfall. The camouflage of nothing the old man wore as his armour, broke down into the idol of the moon, in whose cloak (his own shadow and reflection) the enemy appeared. Long ghostly armies all clad in the light of the moon—the wrinkled face of the lizard—camouflage of sky. This was followed by the march of the stars in whose cloak—idol and reflection—the enemy came. Arrows of light upon the armour of the lizard. Each idol (camouflage of fear) served to block the road to the village of home. "Huntsmen," the old man cried, "our ancient enemy."

"Fishermen", Couvade thought, "our native village."

At long last the retreat began. Was it retreat of enemy or retreat of friend? The idol of the moon fell from the sky. The idol of the stars began to fade. The long ghostly armies crept across the blanket of tribes, the blanket of Couvade sound asleep in his hammock. And in the mouth of the cave where he dreamt he lay since the night his parents ran from the tribe, he too seemed to be passing into the light of freedom—a new sobering reflection—bridge of relationships.

Bridge of dawn upon which the feather of the day and the feather of night danced: bridge of dawn upon which enemy and friend, hunter and hunted, embraced: bridge of dawn upon which the net of his mother and the cloak of his father whirled in a ballet over the Place of the Toucan, the Place of the Fish. Whirled like a hill of dust—a net of stars—a flock of memories—as he, Couvade, shook himself lightly, danced on tiptoe towards the wall of the cave—the bridge of tribes—the bridge of dawn.

And yet because of his grandfather's warnings and rebukes he was still uncertain. Uncertain that the battle of idols, camouflage and armour, was over. Uncertain of the figures coming alive on the wall of the cave. Uncertain there was not a long hard way to go before the idols and paintings would truly melt, truly live, birth of compassion, birth of love. Uncertain he would not have to go around again in a great circle—dress and undress, sprinkle himself with dust, travel-stain himself, play the role of both enemy and friend. Uncertain of the riddle of the night—the riddle of his name.

For with the ascent of the sun it was as if all his uncertainties arose and the bridge of dawn—the dance of the feathers— melted: became the siege of dawn—siege of the bridge of dawn —siege of the tribes, long endless retreat. The lizard suddenly ran, (WAS HE FOE OR FRIEND?) ran along the bars of Couvade's hammock. Ran like the law, the law of earth, very wily, very cautious, the warning of the law: ran like love, the love of heaven, very gay, very relaxed, whimsical and open. It was the old wrinkled face of the trickster of the tribe—half-law, half-love—looming above him. Waking him. The wizened arms of the trickster lifted him as if he were a child again, as if his parents had just vanished, leaving him hidden in the mouth of the cave. The wizened arms lifted him—aged camouflaged arms—THE BRIDGE OF THE AGED—all bones and skeletons. Lifted him again upon THE BRIDGE OF THE CHILDREN— threadbare camouflaged arms. Took him sternly and warningly to his breast—namesake camouflage—THE BRIDGE OF NAMES. Then on into the village as if he were once again a prisoner of the tribe from whom his parents had fled. Fled from the stern tribe who claimed him (Couvade) as a huntsman of night, the child hidden by his erring parents before their flight.

His grandfather knew they had broken the law of *couvade*, the law of the fast, eaten meat and fish. He had seen them dance when dancing was forbidden. The Song of the Fish and the Song of the Feather—both forbidden. The Song of the Net and the Song of the Cloak—both forbidden. He had seen them run laughing The Race of the Feathers when racing was forbidden. He had seen all this, following them secretly. He had watched them hide the child in the cave of ancestors and had taken him up in his arms, his own grandson, Couvade.

"You are the last in a long line of huntsmen of night," the old man said. "I shall call you Couvade. You must learn caution. You must learn not to break the law."

"*Fishermen* of night," Couvade said pleadingly. "In the beginning you said we were fishermen of night." He recalled the shining net of his mother and the dark cloak of his father, both of which the old man had wrenched from him.

But the old man said, "I was mistaken. The fishermen of night are now our enemies. They live to the west of us. We must beware of their tricks. We must watch. We must listen." His voice echoed in the cave of ancestors and faded. . . .

AT THAT MOMENT COUVADE GLANCED UP AND THERE, HIGH IN THE ROOF OF THE PAINTED CAVE, THE LIZARD SMILED DOWN AT HIM. ITS EYES LOOKED VERY FRIENDLY AND VERY WISE. IT GAVE ITS HEAD A SLIGHT SHAKE AS MUCH AS TO SAY, "FISHERMEN OF NIGHT, HUNTSMEN OF NIGHT, PLACE OF THE TOUCAN, PLACE OF THE FISH, EAST, WEST, ENEMIES, FRIENDS". Then IT FLICKED ITS TAIL LIKE THE FEATHER OF THE TOUCAN AND SPOKE.

"The name you bear," the lizard said to Couvade, "means *sleeper of the tribe*."

And it vanished.

I, Quiyumucon

NOTE

By *Quiyumucon* the Caribs meant *First Cause* or ancestral time. The stages by which this assumption was reached are not disclosed in the scanty historical or mythological records available to us though these are stamped in places by a luxuriant imagination and sense of poetry.

Poli, son of *Quiyumucon*, is an invention.

I have attempted to see *Quiyumucon* through the subjective eyes of the late twentieth century as painted Rock-King or ancestor whose association with his people reflects a tradition of sacrifice steeped in uncertain origins and convulsive landscapes, earthquake and volcano.

The records of the Caribs disclose that they were a proud and fierce people with a terrifying sense of order accompanied by a profound ambivalence—guilt and melancholy. There are many speculations as to the land which they originally possessed, and their departure—which was the first step they were to make towards extinction—remains obscure.

Some say their original homeland was Brazil, others Florida and so on. It is known that they mastered the sea—named after them—across which they sailed in Viking formation. They have also been identified with the legendary battledress of the women of the Amazon.

The introduction of a Carib warrior maiden or Queen in this story, therefore, is mythologically consistent though—according to history—the Caribs did not bring their women with them but married their prisoners, Arawaks and others. As a result two or more languages were spoken in the tribe, one by the rulers or men—another by the ruled or women.

Note

My fable of a First Cause or causeway—blind man's ford—is an imaginative exploration of the deed of conquest in controlling as well as assimilating others.

There is the rudiment of a Carib myth to do with an "egg" of creation which passed from the male to the female and this I have adapted to my own purposes.

I, Quiyumucon

I

Poli, the son of Quiyumucon, ruling ancestor or King, was in his thirteenth year. He loved the ceremonial objects around him and sometimes he adorned himself with feathers or wore the cloak of a jaguar or blew through a hollow branch or tumpet until the leaves of the forest rained upon him. And then in his imagination he sailed within the hammock of the rainbow to the sacrificial rocks of Quiyumucon.

It was a curious half-drowsing thought within which to dwell as I watched the painted figures on the wall in the vaguely flickering lantern light which shone in the cave. I had arrived there that day (in the year 1970) in the heart of the Bush with a party of researchers, intent on reconstructing a model of Carib mythology. Now night was falling. The other members of the party had fallen asleep exhausted on the ground. I, too, was exhausted yet I found myself seeking to concentrate on Poli and Quiyumucon and at first with uncertainty then with increasing awareness felt myself transported to another world. Poli was winking one eye at me with rare humour and sadness. There was the tinkling of a bell like the distant ripple of running water.

"The hammock and rainbow in which I sail," Poli said to me with a sudden dark grave look far beyond his years, "are now bridges of sacrifice though once they were—in the very nature of the elements—part of a circle or globe or egg of creation."

As one who slept—now with the living Carib dead I paid the closest attention to him as the hammock of dreams stirred. Poli was, in fact, addressing me as if I were his father and idol, Quiyumucon.

His voice rang suddenly with the spirit of rebuke—"Why must I sail to the sacrificial rocks? Why is it necessary that I do this? Shall I ever reach there and if I do shall I ever return?"

I did not reply. I felt my lips like Quiyumucon granite, cruel as the law. And yet I felt too the strange tenderness of the sand of blood running from the crevices in the ancient wall of ancestors. Poli was piloting his rainbow hammock, a black mask of hair veiling his eyes and lips which were slits of flame. This character of metamorphosis served to accentuate the mask of his features which at one moment seemed to accept and trust me (as when a little while ago they winked one eye) and at another, as in this instant, seemed to burn with hate.

Tall for his age and slender of limb. If I moved that hair aside, that veil aside, I dreamt, his mother would stand forth like a warrior maiden of old: his mother who had secreted herself at the heart of the male host in their retreat from the land of origins, and it was not until they advanced into an area (lying between Orinoco and the mountains of Guiana) which became their new homeland, that her Amazon disguise was uncovered and from breastplate and hair a woman of pure Carib blood stood forth.

I trembled as I recalled the event as if a bird's egg had fallen from the sky and in place of the sun of creation stood a creature still covered in feathers, half-sinister and lovely as the moon. It was a stroke of genius on her part. She had taken advantage of the chameleon of war—long secretive hair of night and curious hidden breastplate of sun—to insinuate herself into the company without arousing suspicion. In fact she consolidated a ruse, then in its infancy, of shock identification, day that resembled night, night that resembled day, bird that resembled beast, beast that swam like fish, woman who appeared like man, man who appeared like woman, to harass and confuse the enemy in the name of Amazon or Viking.

Poli, therefore, as the son of Quiyumucon and the warrior maiden of old, as the last descendant of pure Carib blood, occupied a supreme position in the Carib heartland. This was made manifest when his mother was killed three months after he was born by an arrow that pierced her hammock and breast as she slept. It was now, as I looked back in time at that sacrificial murder, that I stretched forth my hand with infinite pity to part the mask of hair from Poli's brow (in order to identify him beyond a shadow of doubt as my son, after his long sojourn with the priests)—but he shrank away as if an intuition had entered the very core of his being, an arrow of eclipse shot by the bridegroom of the sun across the hammock of the moon.

2

"You killed her," he said to me. "You killed my mother."

I was struck by a transformation of appearances. The place had darkened and the hand of a priest, sawn off above the wrist and presented now on the arm of a long spear, covered the lantern in the middle of the cave to simulate the shadow of eclipse. In this veiled moment the bell of the stream I had heard when the hammock of dreams first stirred began to pound like a cataract of water. We stood within blind man's ford—the first sacrificial waterfall painted on the wall and before us loomed the other sacrificial rapids like phantoms of order upon a succession of rocks in the dark of the lantern moon.

Poli cried again—"You killed her." I found myself at first unable to reply with the graven lips of Quiyumucon since the metamorphosis of the cave seemed to possess such deadly frightful beauty and earnestness, it flashed not only with the hand of eclipse but with the arrow and rain of spirit. "Yes," I admitted inwardly, "it is true I killed her."

"You murdered her," Poli's voice rang in my ears together with the bell of the stream. I partly wakened then in protest and before I fell asleep again it dawned on me like a consolation that I was party to a dream of ancestral time, standing upon earth's ford of broken celestial water and sky, and Poli's speech was part of a ritual bond and accusation.

I found myself being apprised of the facts. Since the death of his mother he had been in the care and instruction of the Carib priests and this moment—for which he had been schooled beyond his years—was no stranger in time to him. I realized he had been away so long I scarcely knew him at all though he, like myself, was a chosen instrument of the tribe, clay of the psyche.

"I slew her", I said, "in obedience to the command of the priests. And now, my son, come closer. The light is bad. I need to see you better. Listen to me. *You* are alive, *she* is dead." I put forth my hand to lift the black hair painted on the wall but Poli drew back with horror and misgiving.

"Poli", I said strongly, with a note of pleading in my voice, "listen I say. Try to understand. She was the last maiden of our blood—a warrior maiden at that. She helped to forge and consolidate a tradition: the chameleon of war—breastplate and hair."

"You killed my mother," Poli insisted.

"It was a time", I tried to reason with him, "when the Caribs had begun to take as wives the women of a foreign race—Arawaks and others like that. There was great danger that we would be seduced by the soft ways of those we had overcome: wooed away by them from the stern habit of the law. We had to arm ourselves, I tell you, my son, against the guile of our victims. Can you not see this?"

"All I know is that you murdered her," said Poli and he sobbed.

"Poli, *you are our son—mine and hers,*" I cried. "Dry your eyes. Tears belong to the weak. Listen. She was very dear to me. The last Carib maiden I knew. When she was discovered by the host of the tribe none of us at first could believe our eyes. Here was our equal—a warrior maiden—think of that— and as such it was the last marriage I, the King, could consummate with an equal in rank and station—warrior to warrior —like day to day, night to night, before the egg of creation was broken. . . ."

"You slew her with an arrow as she slept. That is all I know."

"As one who was dearest and nearest to me," I urged, taking my stand with Quiyumucon, "the very marrow of my bones," I cried to the hand over the moon, "one who was my day when I chose to be day, my night when I chose to be night, one who therefore knew the unity of the stars, pooled yolk of suns and stars and moons (do you understand?) universal egg, self-eclipse, self-illumination, all one, *all one,* I repeat. . . ." I paused. Poli opened his lips to speak but I rushed on. "She was the last of a perfect line of women, the finest and bravest we knew. Therefore to make a sacrifice of her was to begin to harden our heart—the pooled heart of the tribe—against all who followed—foreign brides, foreign mistresses, since having slain what was closest and best we knew that none (however crafty, however, beguiling however tender) could deceive us and draw us from the path of duty. Can you not see, my son, what an election her death was?"

"Did you look at her?" asked Poli all of a sudden in a soft strangled ominous voice. "Did you look at her face afterwards father?" He spoke the word *father* with a muffled cry that could have been hate or love. I began to tremble then. It was hard to believe that Quiyumucon granite could tremble but I shook as if a far-away earthquake invested the cave.

I knew I had broken the law. I had not parted her hair and robe and looked on her face and breasts as I had been instructed to do by the priests of the tribe. I cupped my hands over my eyes. "No," I told him, "I could not bear to look on one so tender. She was dead. But let me look at you Poli my son. You are alive." I moved the cup from my eyes and though he shrank still farther away from me and I still could not see through his mask—through his hair which fell now as hers fell then—I felt that he smiled secretly and sadly and triumphantly. And that the hand over the moon grew darker still until I could no longer tell if it was he or the ghost of the warrior maiden, his mother, who stood there on blind man's ford.

3

A further metamorphosis of the cave began as the distant tremor and earthquake subsided. The hand of the priest, sawn off at the wrist and extended on the long arm of a spear, covered a lantern sun this time. It was as if I had moved to another sacrificial rock and whereas the first had been an eclipse of the moon, this was an eclipse of the sun. Not—it seemed to me—that the cave was any lighter. It was still blind man's ford on the cataract of the river and the bell of the waterfall still rang at our feet.

Poli had faded into the darkness of the cave but I, Quiyumucon, and the warrior maiden whom I had slain with an arrow, rose now again like grievous stars and constellations of blind day within the eclipse of the sun. She lay on her rainbow hammock, which had been nailed to the faint bark of a tree, scooped and converted into a royal bed or canoe by the priests.

I recalled how I trembled the night I slew her until the granite of which I was made shook like the sea of the sun. I had disobeyed the priests in refusing to lift the veil from her dead face.

Now—upon the shore of eclipse, sacrificial rock—I had been given a second chance. I thought of Poli whose blood would be on my head like an ocean of remorse, epitaph or sea named after us, if I did not obey.

I strove with all my will—a dew of sweat on my brow—but found myself still riveted to the wall. The clamour of wings rose from cataract and river.

And then a thought suddenly came to me. Why should I need to uncover the face of my deed, of my warrior maiden, when the sea of time was at hand to bear it away through and beyond the mirror of eclipse? No need to tremble before a hammock of grief in the shadow of the sun. For surely if this eclipse were such a rainbow of stars like sunrise—bringing back the unwanted mask of the dead—there must be a hidden sunset into which we could sail like the unsculpted yolk of an egg . . . starless ubiquity . . . night?

I recalled the first time we had tried to make our own ritual sunrise and sunset of ancestors within which to embark like shadows of the future. With the dawn of day we used to see a flock of brilliant parrots flying from us towards our ancient homeland far away across the sea. With the coming of night they returned and vanished quickly. We observed them closely and read the scroll of the sky as if it were our own ghostly hand up there in space, deed of eclipse over the race of the sun.

Then it was that I, Quiyumucon, with my heart in my mouth, sought to construct the first bier of time—ship of doom— beyond the hammock of the rainbow. I shot my arrow into space. It pierced the invisible host on the edge of night and one parrot fell, sudden splendid plumage, outstretched wings, sailing within the boat of the sky.

I recalled how I knew I had failed in my plan—how my bier or ship was wrecked even before it had been properly launched —for on securing him, the dead bird, to masthead or bow, the flock materialized and descended towards us confused and violated and wild. It was the first time for them too that a feathered creature, a royal parrot, had been shot from the sky and stitched to the brow of a man painted to harness time to the shadow of his will. They wanted to know whose omniscient wreck of a fleet it was to which their bright trailing feathers were nailed. As they flew around me in a rainbow coloured flag, like a sail on the horizon of night, I wondered whether they would pluck my eyes out of Quiyumucon granite to confirm the wreck of darkness on my brow, sacrificial rocks, blind man's ford.

Poli now reappeared from the shadow of the cave into which he had vanished and as he stood before me I felt he carried within him the dawning seeds of his mother's death.

4

Poli's reappearance was indeed curious. I realised now that it was not simply a question of his moving into or out of the shadow of the cave but that against a deepening tide of eclipse, constellations normally obscure in the paint of the sun began to stand out with the brush of night on day.

The dawning seeds of apprehension I now associated with him, in connection with his mother's death, extended from his brow like a string of beads or stars. Beneath each seed or bead of star I could discern the sprouting outline of a war canoe moored to a sacrificial rock on blind man's ford.

There were several such canoes and they all stood on the tide of history that had branched with the Viking Caribs across a sea of islands and up the rivers of a continent. Each had been built like exploratory vessels of doom, experimental cocoons, voyages into the unknown. They all bore the masthead of Quiyumucon: they all resembled the bier of his Queen, the royal parrot which marked his failure since he had been unable to overshoot the mirror of sacrifice.

They bore also—these war canoes of Quiyumucon—a heap of ornaments or substitutions; long feathers of night, long wigs of hair, breastplates of sunrise and sunset: the chameleon of the Amazon through which the fierce climax of war had rolled as though within a marriage to all creatures and things, still leaving, however, that irresolution of horizon Quiyumucon dreaded.

So no wonder another effort was contemplated, Poli realized, another ship of doom he discerned in construction within the shadow of the last sacrificial rock of all on blind man's ford. The outlines were still unclear at this stage but as he looked from it back to Quiyumucon—as he looked around at the stern but listless Caribs—he was filled with foreboding about himself and his race. It was as if a gigantic reaction had begun to set in at the very peak of conquest, a gigantic dissatisfaction or exhaustion and a sense that time was running out— that it was now or never the bier of ultimates must be built, which would relieve them of confronting the face of their deeds, long since accomplished in the name of order and now worthless as clay, the clay of the psyche Poli felt in the mirror of eclipse.

Poli wondered—with the wisdom of the priests far beyond his years—whether it was a kind of commanding death wish, the death wish of a primitive people, superstitiously impelled by the race of the dead, the mask of the dead, which they must somehow preserve unbroken even if it meant a voyage to extinction.

As he looked closely at the new vessel now under construction he realized there was one element of importance he could not ignore. Clearly there was no intention of using the effigy of the Queen, his warrior mother, as before. Poli saw that Quiyumucon, in disobeying the priests, had deprived himself of the efficacy of his beloved muse for the last voyage he contemplated into the unknown. She (or it) had worked like a magic charm in taking them up to the watershed of victory but this voyage—this new voyage on the other side of the hill—down the ball of the sea through the reflection of memory—demanded the blood of youth to resist every constellation, to resist every trick—a new masthead of generations—a new pride and will—a new instinct for unreflecting and unburdened decision at the helm of things.

This time, Poli saw, his father sought to placate the priests —to perform the spirit, if not the letter, of the law, by unveiling the one to be sacrificed before the actual event.

"No," said Poli and this time there was a tremor in his voice. "The priests are very clear about this father. You cannot unmask a deed before it is done."

And yet even as he spoke he had approached the new vessel in the shadow of eclipse as if to declare himself its future masthead. Here, beyond doubt, his judgement was confirmed: this was no ordinary canoe. Its essential framework was a kind of wreck. This was accentuated by the persistent flag of stars— ring of birds—which sailed where the masthead of the Queen had been and which Quiyumucon had failed to submerge on the horizon of night when he sought to sail into the unsculpted yolk of all—into the most hidden sunset of time—beyond every reflection of memory within the shadow of the sun.

It was this sense of the omniscient wreck of a fleet of darkness that drew Poli to stand on the last deck of all like a living prophetic masthead in place of the muse of Quiyumucon, and to look back towards the other vessels—each moored to its sacrificial rock—as to a fleet in reverse, all participating this unfinished ship, this ultimate deck on which he stood, whose beginnings lay far back in an original deed of memory, an original voyage of conception beyond a homeland which it became so necessary to erase that the Caribs had fled and invested their flight with exotic phrases like 'ship of doom', 'bier of time', anything that would nerve them to an implacable austerity, a living and frightful immediacy purged of reflective consciousness.

I approached the deck on which Poli stood.

"No", said Poli again, like a parrot or oracle drilled by the priests, as I stretched out my hand to lift the hair from his face, "you cannot unmask a deed before it is done."

Ruling ancestor though I was I felt it necessary to explain. "Listen," I said, "you stand where the figure of your mother once stood. I have not told you this before but I was blind to her in her life as I remained to her in her death. When my warriors found her and brought her to me she was wild— painted with feathers—chameleon of war. . . ."

"You made her your bride. You must have seen her then."

"All ceremonial our marriage was, I tell you, more paint and processional. I slept at blind man's ford with a maiden of war. Let me look at you my son." I spoke to him as to an equal.

"I will not," cried Poli.

"Do not hide from me now I say . . ."

"I do not wish to hide father. But the priests have warned and commanded."

I felt a sudden rage. "Priests. Priests. What do they know of action?"

"They know of the action of love father."

"Superstitious love, nothing more, in this Carib sea and sun. We are haunted by it. And since you speak of action my son—it is action which must purge us of the ignorant reflection of love. *The deed is all*. It is useless to pine and look back into the mirror of eclipse. The night I slew your mother I should have come to a compromise with the gods. I should have arranged to unveil her—not after (in the letter of contemplation as instructed) but immediately before (in the spirit of action as intended)—by creeping up on her unawares, moving softly to her hammock while she still slept in the land of the living, though so drugged by the priests as to appear already dead. I should have parted the hair from her face and the armour from her breasts, stripped her of paint and scanned her entirely, scanned the ignorant nature of love, if such there should be, lying there as the naked embodiment of an age. A moment later I could have killed her within a single stroke, sight and execution, as it were, a single round action—do you follow me? —wherethrough in abolishing her I would have abolished the necessity to look on my deed, since the deed was all and *nothing* could remain afterwards."

Poli stood like stone with his hand over his face and as I put forth my hand to grasp him now, to *see* him as I slew him, the hand of the priest over the sun moved in unison with mine, the eclipse faded and he vanished in a blind painting of light . . . I could hear his voice, however, addressing me from the ship of space—or if not space (and this was the strangest thing of all)—from the masthead of the future. It was a terrifying gesture of fulfilment. Had I, in fact, accomplished my own wish—so erased the act from reflection—that he stood there now as the universal deed of light, the unsculpted cross of the sun?

I raised the blind hand now that killed my son and the spear of light pierced me then.

5

The swift spear of dawn had now entered the cave and the warning of the priests Poli had transmitted to Quiyumucon began to make itself clear. It was akin to the shattering blood of the fleet of an age—the almost unbearable thrust of sacrificial fire, rather than a gradual muse and digestion of the face of time.

I was half-awake now but dreaming in blind daylight as if still asleep and as I took my stand with Quiyumucon I observed the wreck of his fleet of darkness as it began to fade back into the growing paint of the sun.

It was a curious reality because in a sense as I observed the passage of his canoes through dazed eclipse into the explosive ruin of light I realized that I, Quiyumucon, had gained my desire but in a manner which contradicted my own shadow when I disobeyed the priests.

This was not the horizon of sunset, hidden sunset I desired, but of sunrise, the blind of dawn within which the stars were extinguished.

The sacrificial play painted on the walls of the cave became a calendar of suns which rose and stretched from the masthead of Poli—backwards from the invisible sunset of the future into the formless sunrise of the past and littoral of home upon which the fading fleet of the Caribs now stood: a curious sale or auction of primitive vessels of guilt which were blending into the sky.

It was the auction of a sea of gold in the present and future whose price of guilt, in the bliss of action, I had not understood as a bonfire of sun . . . it was the auction of the wreck of our fleet through Poli's masthead, bier of light . . . it was the auction of the deed of kith and kin and the blind of nails in that deed—the sun of paint on my hand concealing Poli's blood—through which I began to discern faintly the hand of the priest that moved and retreated like a clock of ancestors in unison with mine.

This—the clock of the Caribs known as Quiyumucon or First Cause—was the most curious shadowy commodity for sale on blind man's ford. For in it and around it lay a causeway of relationships which brought into new focus the disparate canvas of the fleet. There was the Viking hand of ancestor time and the Amazon hand of warrior Queen upon a sea of gold.

The sun blazed in the rubbled face of the clock and this eclipse—the boulder of sun upon sun—possessed its own flakes and shadows, as the eclipse of darkness upon darkness embodied its own stars.

Quiyumucon and Poli were dancing and leaping with the warrior maiden around the rock of the sun and in their shadow or flake lay the heart of the chameleon of the tribe, the rocking clock of ancestors capable of reconciling the ship of doom with the splintered bier of light, the materialisation of fossils in a mirror of eclipse with the dematerialization of darkness in a mirror of suns.

The clock of the ship indeed was a landslide of memory known as First Cause, the causeway of the blind. And it was this deed of the sky which first set the bell tolling at the heart of the cataract like a grievous living blow administered by Quiyumucon within which the first shadow of time, curtain or waterfall, mourned and justified its existence.

In addition to the tolling bell now ticked the clock of the rock, pendulum of sky, like a glancing arrow diffused and reflected into the second shadow of time, painted flake or rain of Quiyumucon.

It was a saving reduction of scale to which all things now mourned and danced. The flake of Quiyumucon or First Cause turned to a grain of sand like the shadow of an ant. And this began to pace the numberless hours on the face of nature's clock. Hours that secreted to themselves an infinite reduction of the fantastic march of events through the landslide of the sun.

Although the masthead of Poli had once been the top of a living mountain blasted by the lightning of Quiyumucon and as the deed of the sky ran to the sea, sweeping all in its path, Poli became the receptacle of the forces of the land which streamed through him—except that, in the shock of translation, his was a basket or sieve which retained but a shadow of memory, the shadow of sand as the dance of history.

This it was, this dance of scale, that became the balancing role in which I was now absorbed as though I created it all in the very camouflaged beginning when from original chameleon (known as the mountains of Poli) the Caribs were first expelled. These mountains and valleys had been their controversial place in the paint of the sun; and the sacrificial rocks of Quiyumucon (First Cause or Sky) and Poli (mast of earth) were my recapitulation of that lightning feud and expulsion— ultimate fleet—wreck of darkness—endless beginning of beginnings—first causes within undisclosed movements.

The enemy who returned to fulfil a sacrificial role in driving or launching them forth were distant relatives of Quiyumucon claiming equally to be the first tenants of the land expelled in their turn long long before. They came in such superior numbers now that Quiyumucon and his people were taxed to the utmost to defend themselves. And it was then that they began to practise what was to become their ultimate strategy of offence and defence (enigma of war)—the art of metamorphosis which in addition to employing the paint of feathers or the stripes of animal, the breastplate of day or the long hair of night, knew how to advantage itself within a curious reduction of the scale of events.

The camouflage of the ant was first employed to fantasticate into irrelevance the superior numbers of First Tenant now back on the doorstep. He (Quiyumucon) so secretly deployed his forces he was everywhere and nowhere, everything and nothing and this began to wear the enemy down until they were convinced they were involved in a campaign which dissipated their strength, destroyed their morale, wasted their fibre and ate into their reserves like a familiar disease: diseased projection into no one and nothing.

Quiyumucon succeeded in paralysing the enemy for a while until a sheer cliff of numbers coming up from the rear drove him up the masthead of Poli which he held, extending his command into a certain valley whose starved watercourse and environs at this time of the year were known by various names such as the lap of war, the maiden of war, the ship of war.

Then it was a certain inspiration flashed in his mind—a new reduction of scale—his fleet or ship of oblivion. It was time, he decided, to break free fom the mountains, descend the valley into the sea, embark for another land, a foreign land, a foreign conquest. This would entail a new trigger, a new trap, a deed of soul to invest both valley and sea. Where the campaign of the ant appeared before like a reduction of numbers, the ship of scale must adapt all things into its camouflage, a silent sea upon which to sail across the land, a silent fish within which to dive through the land, silent beasts upon which to ride in the land—silent forests within which to move—silent birds through which to fly—charmed concert of stillness through and beyond the earthquake of war, the fire voices of the enemy.

Those fire voices crackled and sang and burned closer night after night, day after day, and Quiyumucon felt himself ringed by a fever of hate. He longed for an end and a new unmoved yet farflung beginning—a climate of conquest and extinction where he needed but the shadow of kinship abreast his soul. It was a primitive obsession, a primitive disease, an obsession with sight and execution, sacrificial constellation.

The priests had supported him in the camouflage of the ant but they warned him against his new venture, ship of scale. It might prove precipitate and dangerous but Quiyumucon hardened his will.

He put his men to work and soon the hatred of the enemy turned to amazement though the intention of it all—such amazing craftmanship—they could not fathom: it was not the alien Horse of Troy nor the fiery Cross of Spain which rose to confront them but a fleet of Magical Canoes built with infinite skill like a fantastic rehearsal of a play of sacrificial rocks—blind man's ford—in the cave of dreams. Except that at this stage of rehearsal in the migration of the Caribs—valley of creation—the mastheads chosen were neither those of Poli nor the warrior maiden though, in fact, the mountains stood overhead in anticipation of a future voyage back into the paint of the sun and the valley itself in which the vessels grew, deck by deck, line by line, was like a giant ship itself or lap of war.

There were, first of all front-line vessels of the jaguar, so built they appeared ready to spring at a moment's silence. They were moored to a trigger of rock. And sometimes in the starved watercourse where they lay like vertical horizons or sprung hammocks weighing the sky, the slip knot of lightning stiffened at either end presaging the fixed rains to come across the valley of time.

In the second line stood vessels of the forest so built they looked like trees ready to walk, to blossom fire at a moment's silence. They were moored to skeleton rock. And sometimes in the starved watercourse where they stood, they leaned like the charmed antlers of the land festooned with fossil palm and the rust of orchids presaging the fixed hail to come across the valley of time.

57

In the third line stood vessels of cloud so built they looked like birds of storm ready to fly at a moment's silence. They were moored to the cloud of rock. And sometimes in the starved watercourse where they rested they looked like the silent race of the wind whose spirit of evaporation was the quicksilver of action presaging the fixed vapour to come across the valley of time.

In the fourth and last line stood vessels of the fish so built they looked like the very scales of earth. And these—unlike the first three lines which were sparked to spring however still the dream of action—were anchored to the very heart of unconsciousness (earth's dive or motion) presaging an ocean of space to come though the fixed rains ran and the fixed hail fell and the fixed vapour blew.

As the four lines of the fleet appeared the enemy looked and wondered but could not fathom their relative function and intention. Yet they were held, as it were, by the hand of magic as though the moorings which held the various craft drew them, too, into orbit, fixture of rain and hail and cloud. It was an elaborate and compelling mission of beauty and skill.

They were aware all the time—during the spell of construction—that such a fleet could not dream to embark until the river rose to its full height. Quiyumucon read their hearts, First Tenants of the Land. He knew they would bide their time, fiends nursing ambition, until the vessels were finished. Then they would descend, armed to the teeth, to appropriate the spoil: such wealth as they had never imagined—the fixed boat of creation—beasts, forests, clouds, birds—the fleet of time.

Quiyumucon knew, as one conversant with the deeds of the sky, the very hour the river would rise and the elements come. He set his trap and the enemy, dumbfounded at their opportunity—everything ready and finished now—began to descend into the river.

Quiyumucon, safely positioning himself on the mountains of heaven, laid his ritual charge of sunrise, explosive hail, rain, wind, to the masthead of Poli, the ship of the valley. The priests sought to restrain him but he was adamant. It was a sacred mountain, they said, born of the sky and the maiden of earth. It was First Cause, they said. But Quiyumucon hardened his heart against them all, sacred and profane, conflicting causes. He was determined to trigger his fleet, sacrificial enemy in friend, tenant's hand within tenant, crew of originality in time . . . *and set sail.* . . .

As the First Tenants of the valley (as the enemy called themselves) boarded creation's camouflage Quiyumucon struck. Some say it was not he, after all, whose dive into silence it was but a god's hail of the fathomless moorings and lightning of man.

Others, that it was a god's rain of the swiftest sound and music of man, unplumbed earth, in which the stillest fleet set sail.

Whatever it was Quiyumucon had not been misled by the oracles of despatch through the spoil of war.

The priests said it was his act of disobedience which matched everything, lightning and sound, rain and hail, masthead of the deeps, sea of silence—but he (Quiyumucon) believed it was sight and execution, spirit and intention rolled into one primitive configuration.

As the masthead of Poli snapped and fell Quiyumucon waited, knowing it all already in his heart like the lance of a dream: the new hands he had enlisted in his fleet.

As the first rubble of the deed of the sky fell he saw the first line of vessels stir. The enemy on the deck were so astonished they grew dumb with fascination akin to the beasts they rode and this concert or trigger nerved them to spring on the lancehead of the jaguar through their own gloating plot or desire for the spoil of earth.

Quiyumucon waited and watched. It was a propitious sacrifice, a propitious beginning and end to greed and cruelty. As the second wave and rubble of the deed of the sky fell he saw the second line of his fleet stir and the antlers or vessels of the forests sprang like horns of silence upon which the bodies of the enemy grew still beyond every semblance of desire. It was a passive ornamentation of the hand of his fleet like a caveat of soul in the heart of the future.

Quiyumucon waited and watched. As the third wave or rubble from the deed of the sky fell he saw the third line of his fleet stir like the quicksilver of storm whose annihilation of the lusts of spoil—birds of storm—froze their blood at the same time into a rain of silver wrought upon the wing of each ship. It was a mute cloak or extension into a new world, silent as the gleam of tears.

Quiyumucon waited and watched. As the fourth and last wave fell, the last of his vessels stirred. And now it was as if fire itself broke loose within every hand, clock of sacrifice, but, in fact, the vessels of this line, beyond all others, were chained to death, the endless death of death, the endless beginning of beginnings. Chained therefore to life, link of reflection, Carib boat of the unconscious.

As the massive deluge charged—across line upon line of ship, electric creation—the earth-fish dived and stood, scale of rain, scale of cloud like a knife-edged balance within the rage of the spoil, fused enemy and friend, spiritual tenant . . . .

I woke now in the eye of the Quiyumucon sun which streamed into the cave.

Yurokon

NOTE

Yurokon *serves in this story as a gateway between Carib* and Christian ages. His appearance as the Bush Baby in Carib mythology— the child of the vessel (the Caribs are noted for their beautiful pottery) —coincided both with a fall from sovereign time and dominion, and with the arrival of Columbus.*

The charges of cannibalism levelled against them by Spain, whom they resisted fiercely step by step, appear to have been trumped up by her to justify her own excesses and to be largely untrue, though it is clear from mythological relics such as bone or flute, fashioned from their enemies, that the Caribs ate a ritual morsel—"transubstantiation in reverse" as Michael Swan puts it.

The plastic myth of Yurokon *appears to me to possess so many hidden features (innocence as well as guilt) that I have attempted to portray it as the threshold to a catholic native within whom resides an unwritten symphony—the disintegration of idols as well as an original participation of elements.*

*The word "Carib" is a corruption which became synonymous with "cannibal": Columbus spoke of Caripunas, Raleigh of Carinepagotos, French explorers of Galibis.

Yurokon

I

The Indian reservation of the valley of sleep lay in an open savannah of the Interior. Stunted bush and occasional trees dotted this savannah—miles long and wide—between the mountains where a great forest began and rolled endlessly to the sea. From this naked distance—in the middle of the valley— these forests appeared like black surf of painted cloud. Yurokon had once or twice crossed them to come to the sea. It was a far way off but his memories were intimate and vivid like newly minted letters of space, a harmony of perspectives.

The sun was up when he succeeded in raising his kite. Soon —by judicious tugs—pulling in and paying out of twine—the kite caught a current of air and rose steadily and swiftly into the sky.

He was around fourteen (so the records said); his sister, who had accompanied him, about ten. They were both small of stature, frail of limb, reputed to be amongst the last survivors of an ancient tribe now called *huntsmen of bone*. They possessed a curious air, devoid of age it seemed—animated matchsticks, smouldering a little, quiescent a little. It was the rapidity of their gestures accompanied by an inherent stillness, a silent relationship. And yet it was as if volumes of time existed between them and words of music fell ceaselessly from their lips.

They appeared now half-asleep on earth as the match of space began to slumber. And when their uncle appeared through one

E   65

of the trees they were glad to relinquish the kite to him which he secured to the branch of a tree. Yurokon slid to the ground and watched uncle and sister vanish through a hump of land into the houses of the reservation.

They would return, he knew, with food and drink. He lay against the trunk of a tree and could not bear to leave his kite which he glimpsed through the leaves as it slept on a cloud —and bore him up into a skeleton of light through the valley of sleep.

"Are we really huntsmen of bone?" Yurokon asked, looking down at his uncle and through the sky as he sailed in space. For it was as if the blue trunk of the ocean stood there whittled down to a cross, coral and bone, octopus in whose blood ran tin, sponge in whose crevices ran gold.

"We became huntsmen of bone when we ate our first Spanish sailor," his uncle replied to the intricate sticks of the sky. "For that reason we are sometimes called cannibals." He looked sardonic, his left eyebrow cocked in quizzical fashion, pointing still to the kite, paper of heaven nailed to wood.

"Cannibals," said the boy, startled. "I don't see why anyone should call us that."

It was Easter in the Indian reservation of the twentieth century and Yurokon had been given a kite by a visiting missionary, which sailed through the book of space and continued in his sleep in pages of psyche; coral and gold.

"For that reason we are sometimes called cannibals," the man repeated, pursuing his own thread of thought backwards into time. "We ate a Spanish sailor. . . ." He was jealous of the missionary and wished to distract his nephew, glued to space.

"How can you say such a thing?" Yurokon cried, descending from kite to earth in a flash and stopping dead, riveted now to the ancient trunk of man, the lines and brow, the anchor of subsistence.

They stood under a small tree in the valley of sleep and Yurokon observed a spectral nest hanging from one of its branches; to that bough also he saw had been tied the thread of his kite which he had ascended and descended on scales of light. "It's chained there," he cried as if he had forgotten whether it was the missionary or his uncle who had done it, "chained to nest and branch."

His uncle nodded to a silent tune, and reaching up into the nest drew forth a thin bone or flute. He passed it over his lips without making a sound, polished it between the palms of his hands and after this palaver with the dead gave it to Yurokon who blew, in his turn, a sad yet vibrating melody of space. All at once he could hear and feel running through his hands the giant tremor of that bird, the ladder of the pilot, as it flew soundlessly through the sky chained to the earth.

He could hear also an unwritten symphony: the dark roots in the past of that tree—a strange huddle of ancestral faces attuned to quivering wings which they plucked with their fingers like teeth. And then silently, as if for the first bitter time, tasted the fear of the strings: ascent and descent: transubstantiation of species: half-tender, half-cruel, like a feast.

They read it, in their mouths, on the craft of Spain—the curious cross of a bird which flew towards them across the sea: crane or pelican or flag. It might even have been their first fleshless pirate, skull and crossbones of the fleet, harp of flesh.

"Do you mean?" said Yurokon as the first wave of magical numbers struck him, "that it was a game to make them think they had been eaten . . . ?" He stopped, aware of a waking plight in the valley of sleep, the plight of feeling akin to non-feeling, flesh akin to spirit.

"In a manner of speaking, yes," said his uncle approvingly. "*Make them think they had been eaten*. Make them into a song of spirit: a morsel in our mouths, nothing more, the morsel of the flute, that was all." He waved his hand nonchalantly.

Yurokon nearly spat the flute from his mouth as though suddenly it burnt his tongue like fire, immortal burn, immortal skin, immortal native, immortal cannibal. He began to age into the ancient Child of Legend. It was a story he had been told from the beginning—that he was the last Carib and the first native. . . .

2

Yurokon appeared centuries ago in the valley of dreams as the native heaven of tears and laughter, of carnival and guilt when the revolution of conquest was over.

His uncle was expecting him and though he barely discerned the spiral of smoke-like twine coming up out of the pot on the fire, he felt the sting of fire—tears of a match.

It was here in this sky of election—bastard soil—cannibal legend—that the song of the kite was born.

"Make them think it was a marriage of spirits, laughter of the feast," his uncle said languidly, with the glaze of the pot in his eye.

"I am your brother's spirit," said Yurokon and there was a responsive glaze in his mood or brow, a god-like rebellious look.

"Which one?" his uncle said flippantly to the devil of the fire. "Brother oh brother."

Yurokon bowed his head to conceal the ash of many a war feast, sculpture of blood. His uncle had many brothers—some had eaten the symbol of deity. "How can we", he said to his uncle, and the words bit his tongue, "be the first natives when they were here before us—I mean your brothers' Arawak wives—my mother's people. . . ?"

"They're our base of time in the light of Spain," his uncle said secretively as though he reasoned with insurrection in his ranks. "No one before us has made this claim—don't you see? —this black morsel". . . . He stirred industriously over the cooking pot and gave a sardonic shrug. "It's our last weapon, our first election. In future, come who or what may, this distinction will stand. It will swallow us all for we, too, will succumb."

"Succumb," said Yurokon and he almost laughed at his fate. "Yet here am I", he cried accusingly, "no one and nothing, yet here I stand. Whose fault is it? Whose spirit is it that will not —*cannot*—die?"

"Child," said his uncle with a gleam that might have been fear, "it is true that the revolution of conquest is over but *you* —your rebellious feud of spirit goes on." He turned away from the glaze of the pot; the hunger of kinship was opening at his feet, twine of blood, twine of water, twine of guilt ascending and descending: flint of savage: skeleton of light.

Yurokon held the twine in his hands as if with a snap, a single fierce pull, he would break it *now* at last. Break the land. Break the sea. Break the savannah. Break the forest. Break the twig. Break the bough. The unwritten symphony of the wind, unwritten spark of the wind, made him bark—a sudden bark. His uncle stared at the bristling dog of the fire, fire break, fire bark, delicacy, magic; he smacked his lips and the roast of Yurokon's bark subsided into the silent bay of conscience like an invocation at the heart of the feast: man's best enemy or friend.

Was it the immortal dog of war and peace that sang in the break of the fire, shadowy tail or bone?

Its voice could be heard in the lull of the wind across the valley of sleep. First the subtlest crash of a symphony, staccato fire, forest tail or bay of the moon in the sky.

Second a hoarse thump which came from a falling tree, surf or tail of the moon.

It was the music of ignominy, ignominious conceit, or so it seemed to Yurokon (his own desire to break everything) on his long march across time into the rebellion of eternity. A long march in which the tail of his kite drew a line across the ash of the sky, camp fire or ghost settlement. A line of demarcation, the frontier of sleep, huntsmen of bone, the song of silence.

It was equally the music of origins upon a trail that lay in all the wild warring elements. First, *broken water*. His uncle possessed an enormous cauldron which he filled with water and set on the fire. Yurokon beheld the dog of his skin soon bubbling there like a cataract of eternity: boiling water which had been innocent before—innocent, that is, as one's own sovereign blood, but now had become the executioner at the feast, native to blood.

Second, *broken fire*. His uncle possessed an enormous spit, a cauldron of fire: as though the sun stood over the valley on a misty morning and began to break its own vessel of intensity through an autumn sunset turning into a tropical, ritual sunrise. So that the steam of the valley appeared to infuse the light, and water boiled fire rather than fire boiling water.

Yurokon saw himself aloft in this cauldron of fire as a dog-kite; the twine connecting him to earth—kite to earth—had been cut by scissors of mist. He stood, therefore, high up as if without anchor or support save that the nape of his neck had been caught by fingers of fire: fingers of a god which had been innocent before—innocent as one's sovereign flesh, but now had become an executioner at the feast, native to flesh.

At this moment on the trail beholding water and broken fire, he looked backwards and forwards at the combat of heaven: immortal outcast, outcast of participation, innocence and guilt. Heaven lay both within and without the things and the people he had taken for granted, and the kite of deity had, on one hand, consolidated—as uncle hinted—a base of time, an election of time to swallow all ages and men; but, on the other, had equally inspired a curious break within the anatomy of the feast—a spiritual hunger and rebellion whose consequences would reveal the inmost vessel or nativity of fate, song of fate.

He had passed through broken voices of water and fire. Now broken atmosphere lay before him like the breath on his lips fried thin as a wafer, flat as a leaf. And so when he moved he began to fly with the feud of air into broken distances: broken water and fire cooked into walls of space by leaves of wood as though water and fire were cold and wood and leaf were hot: wood and leaf which had been innocent before—innocent as nature, but now had become the kite of distance, native to sovereign execution, death-in-life, life-in-death.

Fire. Water. Air. They were all, in a sense, the weapons of a savage dreaming time on a trail where *once upon a child* everything had slumbered on a leash like a victorious shroud but now had become the cauldron of heaven which the huntsmen of bone had not foreseen when they appointed themselves the cannibal or ogre of place to fashion both their catholic native and repulsive sack of the seasons.

That the leash would become the easter twine of endless participation through an immortal outcast, and that the repulsive stocking or sack of the seasons would invoke stomach upon stomach of consumption whose hideousness would be reflected in a deeper and deeper childlike pool of innocence (ogre of water, boiling fire)—raw material of the elements— none had foreseen as the undying birth of freedom. . . .

For it was as if—just as angelic blood was consumed by cannibal water—fire by an atrocity of wood—broken savage time lay, too, within its native soil eternity.

Yurokon was approaching a bend in the trail and he saw both the shroud and sack of the seasons before him. The shroud may well have been a caul such as certain children are born with. The sack or stocking may well have been the pillow of conquest, Eiger in Roraima, snow of the Alps in the Andes in the Amazon. He could now hear the gift of a symphony in the silent bed of earth—black-out shroud of vision, white-out stocking of translation. He had heard the missionary on the reservation speak of the Polar North as an organ of fire it was so cold. Yurokon believed and accepted this paradoxical truth as much as he trusted the song of himself in the sorrow of the bone and the flute—the ages of man—valley of desolation.

"Once upon a child," the shroud said to him advancing along the trail like the dance of the black keys of earth.

"Once upon a time," the sack said to him advancing along the trail like the dance of the white bones of earth.

Yurokon hopped to the white bone and the black flute. He could see clearly now, with the eye of his kite, the ballet of the Caribs as they stubbornly withdrew within the music of the centuries upon the skull-and-crossbones piano of age. At each camp fire they grew extinct in the ash of reflection, but were born again within involuntary pillow or shroud, caul of vision.

Yurokon stepped upon these keys of birth-in-death— broken water and broken fire—black-out . . . white-out . . . ash of earth which he rode like a ladder into the sky.

3

The ladder of the trail ran up into the mountains. And each day as the Caribs withdrew into the clock of the centuries they painted the blue sea falling away beneath them in an underworld picture, an underworld kite which flew in the broken sky of conquest. Flew under their feet upon a rope of ash which descended through knotted stations of fire where the burnt relic of each day's march was buried. It burnt itself there— imagination of a continent—rope and kite—ladder of ascent, and they drew the sea upon their pots and vessels—something fantastically small (a drop of ocean)—something immensely wide which began to consume them at the grassroots of innocence like a cauldron of fury.

The sea-kite possessed many shapes and colours, some gay, some sombre. Some—like the octopus—amused the huntsmen. It made them almost enjoy the innocent malady of the gods since unholy, holy evil was reputed to have a stomach of mail which drank tin.

"Once upon a child," said the stomach of mail to the conscience of the tribe, namely Yurokon, "you ate me," and it tangled its tail and rope around him on the ladder. His uncle laughed, and his sister, taking pity on him, grabbed the octopus by the bones of the kite and ran a little way off across a wave of land to give him room to coax it back into the air.

Another kite, which rose in the underworld sky at his feet, resembled a sponge and this, too, was an endless model of diversion. When the battle of conscience drew it, infinite drops of gold splashed on the ground from the heart of the pelican.

"Once upon a time," said the sponge to the pelican, "I flew in the sea with wings of bone."

In addition to the kite of the octopus and the kite of the sponge there flew a kite of coral, a submerged reef crossed with ritual cousins, related to the sponge, calendrical mosaic, music. It curved and dwindled in shallows and deeps, skeleton of the sea, harp of the feast from which a stringed sound issued, fossil of cloud.

Far beneath the ladder of the mountains the ocean crawled within itself, ribs of bone splashed by huntsmen of shadow. Yurokon observed in the middle of that kite of ocean a loop of burning paint. This was the cauldron of the kite within which octopus and coral and sponge, innocent evil and maleficent good, were living morsels of divinity in their native organ. The laughter dried on his lips—flute of bone—and he tasted instead plankton or euphausiid harnessed to blood: harnessed to the urchin of the sea, spiked hedgehog or jealous god of ocean. This spiky pattern upon the cauldron of the kite reflected the jealous sky of the sea—the brittle constellations and stars, prickly sea-lilies, sea-cucumbers set in a mosaic of fossil and keyboard of ancestors. As though the spiky music of the urchin of stars, the election of the first native of earth, drew one deeper and deeper into a furnace of innocence, consumption of guilt.

Yurokon was the hedgehog of the land, Carib land-urchin to Spanish sea-urchin. He could bark and bristle on the land as if fire were his natural element, sea-dog of night, and with the fall of darkness he no longer flew the sea-kite under him, but rather the land-kite over him.

He imagined himself standing upon the shore of the sea with a new boatload of arrivals, looking up with their eyes at a distant campfire of Caribs. The ground was strewn with the dead of battle, but the bone of the kite blazing on the mountains spoke volumes of the savage character of the land, dancing around its flute. It was as if the dance of the bone wished to declare itself after a day of battle—to all who had newly arrived—by a music of silence, spirit of absorption, gaol of flesh.

That absorption reflected the many shapeless kites of Yurokon in the heart of invader as well as invaded. There was the night octopus of the land whose dance differed from the tail of the sea in that the daytime octopus was a morsel of divinity, morsel of the sea, but the nighttime octopus, as it blazed its points far up on the ladder of the land, seemed the very antithesis of the gods: land-urchin's shroud or sack: campfire of bone: trunk or tree on which Yurokon laid his head in the valley of sleep. Each splinter of the dance, seen from the foot of the cross, ladder of the mountains, flared in the match of a dream, matchstick limbs, twine and distance: glimmer of the pointed hedgehog.

4

Yurokon's field was the grain of the land and sea whose seed-time was conscience, battle of eternity.

As the Caribs withdrew across the ridge of the land and began to descend into a continent of shadow, each knot of ash linked them to the enemy. And Yurokon was the scarred urchin of dreams, victor-in-victim; over the centuries he remained unageing (ageless) as a legend, a curious symptom or holocaust of memory, whose burnt-out stations were equally embryonic as a cradle, fugue of man, unchained chain of fires.

It was this that drew the Caribs to the end of their age. They ceased to fret about names since namelessness was a sea of names. They ceased, too, to care about dwindling numbers since numberlessness was native to heaven, stars beyond reckoning.

The tree, in fact, against which Yurokon slept was known as the tree of name and number. And there were two paths which led to it from the mountains around the valley. The first was called *the ladder of the geese*. It was a game Yurokon had designed in which he dreamt it was all happening the other way around. The mountains were paper—flat as a map. The valley was above, sailing kite, and the barnacle geese which flew towards him rose from paper to kite: hatched not from eggs like other birds but from sea-shell into land-fish, orphans of the globe. For they, too, like Yurokon, were an ageless omen, Good Friday's meat, fish rather than fowl. None grieved for them save Yurokon who accounted himself sibling to a shell— sibling to a fast—as uncle accounted himself guardian to a morsel.

It was the true name of the geese, the true number of the fast which baffled all men. Yurokon drew the flight of the geese as currents or arrows against the shadow of continents —gulf stream or orphan of masses, equatorial current or orphan of hemispheres.

"Barnacle currents," he thought. Wing by fin the land-fish flew—the souls of a drought, the fast of the drowned—waters under the earth.

The valley of sleep had been taken by assault—the fiercest savannah fire of living memory; so swift had it been, all were killed who were taken unawares. Stunted trees remained—bones of grass. Uncle had died, as had Yurokon, in the glare of battle. And now—after three or four years—the scene was re-visited by the Catholic missionary of the Interior, Father Gabriel. It was he who encircled on a map the charred tree of Yurokon as a new root or mission of psyche, spectral nest, bone and flute: it was Eastertide again.

He had visited the mission and given Yurokon a kite two days before the blaze—had he remained he, too, might have been killed. Now here he was again to make a new start, both defend and attack from within and without. An unorthodox priest he was of Spanish and Indian blood, and a composer of music. He dreamt of a native symphony which would reflect a new organ or capacity, a primitive flowering of faith. It was not inconsistent with the last dream of the Caribs, the dream of Yurokon which haunted him, as it haunted them—annunciation of music at the beginning of the end of an age.

"Sailor," said Yurokon to Gabriel. The priest began to protest. But his voice was muffled in his cloth or vocation. He wanted to say—"I am not your mask or morsel." But instead— like curtain and theatre—he let the faceless robe of God descend; Yurokon set aside the flute from his lips and placed collar or shell to his ear.

There were two ladders (Yurokon remembered) leading to

the robe of name and number. The first called tree of the barnacle goose, the second simply *hemispheres: shell of the spheres.*

Yurokon kept the shell to his ear until arrows of rain evoked
an abstract pitch, volume within line. The music he now
heard was both hollow and full, sea-fast, land-fast. When the
sea fasted, it still climbed into the rain of the land: land-fish,
Good Friday's arrow.

Yurokon could hear her sing—his sister who ran before him
now through the day of the battle of the savannah—arrow of
fire—when mail or flame swept on. As though in the singing
theatre of God, history re-enacted itself. . . .

The fire voices came from everywhere and Yurokon woke
to the voice of the tree in which he slept.

He was rooted, in that moment, in fire—as his sister ran
before him with the singing kite of the savannah—fiery attack,
fiery defence.

In the grain of that field of battle—open to conscience—
open to sun—an omen resided, multiplications of grace, zero
as well as fulfilment. This was the logic of Father Gabriel—the
open book of the centuries: annunciation of the native of the
globe.

And now—as his sister ran before him—Yurokon saw a
chain of fires (formerly ash, unchained chain of divinity) but
linked or aligned to him now beneath his robe.

He recalled the naked campfires of his forebears whose arrows
swarmed on the brink of a continent like currents of ocean
barnacled to land.

They were lit, he remembered, as the first grim tide of
welcome to the flag of the pelican. They were equally an offen-
sive/defensive swarm, blazing at the door of the land—sponge
of the sea—blood of gold: blazing ribbon of coastline, legend
or sponge.

He recalled the fierce battles that raged day after day; the retreat that followed night after night, the fatalistic withdrawal into hedgehog and mountain.

The chain of fires along the roof of the coast was the first curiously horizontal phase, therefore, in a vertical war—a vertical cloak or retreat which Yurokon encompassed at this stage as the shroud of the land-urchin over the sea-urchin, land-kite over the sea-kite, night over day.

It was a slow and long pull, he recalled, from the sea to the crest of the land, but they drew their train after them up the mountains, braced themselves in the current of the wind, wing to fin, bone to sack, goose to hemisphere—fast of name and number, tree of camouflage, feast of camouflage, trail of campfires in a single line or uninterrupted break of terror.

One last crackling glance back at the sea-kite from the sky-ridge of the mountains where they stood; he could see them again as they leaned forward, reluctant, sad, and drank a toast (farewell to namesake sea) lip to bowl, lip to the engraving of Spain (and all who came after, bowl of England, saucer of France, vessel of Holland): they engraved it on their lips—primitive fire or callous—like an animal's protuberance, mouth of the sun whose tongue ran with them as they descended the other flank of the mountains—away from the sea—into the lap of the land.

Half-way down they looked back with Yurokon's eyes, and saw her standing there—Sister Fire—Viking Amazon. Her eyes met theirs as she turned from the flank of the sea to the cloth of land. And this time Yurokon felt the parenthesis of the orphan, sea-shell into robe.

Every protection, nevertheless, seemed precarious to him now as the battle of ridge and flank, forest and savannah rolled on: as though his own sister possessed a chain of ambivalences—a menacing outwardness as well as inwardness, unearthly stillness chained to storm, locked propensity, locked voices of fury.

He could see them—his forebears of bone—with their chain of flesh and spirit across the land. They had crossed the naked flank of the sea into the vessel of the forest and now— as they descended into species of Bush and Savannah—Yurokon was aware of the intensity of the flame they drew with them, which like vase or pottery in a rage of colour, signified an acute vice in themselves, blaze or furnace.

He had never been aware of it quite so strangely before— the flimsy scaffold of the robe, shroud of name and number, urchin of the stars, caul of birth, which—like ash—night-kite over day-kite, could mercifully fall to release the chain; or like earth, in the hands of a wise potter, could unlock the vice; but which (in the fold of that vice, colour of fire) broke, for no other clear reason but to instil terror: as if—in breaking—it had not broken at all, save to clinch an outer flesh to an inner mould, an outer fire to an inner blow.

It was this inner blow which, despite the appearances of hell, drew Yurokon back to prize the ash—not as the holocaust it seemed to be, but as the robe of mercy it originally was, parenthesis of the orphan.

Nevertheless, in withdrawing there, he could still see— within his own glimmering shadow—that the chain of the battle rolled on; the fire voice of the savannah sang close at hand of the flesh and spirit of the tiger which had been joined to withstand (within and without) forces and enemies.

And the voice of the tiger, fire voice, fire vase—in line with sea-flame, mountain flesh, muse of the ridge, toast of ancestors, penetration of flank—instilled terror. And like an apparition of ancient camp fire, it disported its robe or ash, bars of shadow through which its naked sides shone: insane factory of war: jointed engine of battles upon which the cloth of the priest precariously stood—not as the sport of unfreedom, but as a necessary condition, leash of grace.

It was curious (half-comic perhaps, half-tragic perhaps) that, in a sense, this ash (this prison) was the flimsy sponge of nature which alone drank volumes of need; the ill-protected, the ill-served—true voice of the tiger.

True voice of the tiger. It began to sing now with rage and scorn: rage at the conversion of prison: scorn at the factory of grace. And as it sang—in repudiation of the ash of truth—its rage and its scorn were joined to flesh and spirit.

This was the last chain, last repulse of the Caribs in that battle of the savannah, whose commemoration rose in a vase of flame: such music of colour it embroiled the savannah in the sea, the mountain in the valley, forest in scrub: bowl of earth, pottery of earth, toast of the valley by the huntsmen of bone who had drunk before from the bowl of the sea.

Such commemoration of colour—such a draught of sensation—such a feast of sensibility—embroiled all things and species in a breakwater of reflection, stretching from the harp of the sea to the kite of the valley.

That music of paradox began with a bar of shadow—unchained fire—*hiatus* of ordeal as the robe of God, the need of man; followed, however, by the wildest repudiation of that need in the sack of truth: though this very sack or body of rage began to point again, back to itself as to an ironical witness, an unremembered, unacknowledged sibling of truth on both sides of the veil.

For if, in fact, the inner tiger of war repudiated its veil or shadow, there were other species whose storm or sack drew them back without protest to the spirit of placelessness, as to the salt of the sea.

The eel of fire, for example, as it ran into battle, coiled into an eye of relief which could have been a needle of snow. For eye of snow, like barnacle of fire, legendary feather, had been spawned on a distant scaffold—desert or Pole—where it grew like an arrow from a subtle hand mapping the globe.

The bird of species as well, as it flew into battle, spun the feather or the thread in the needle in the very eye of snow. For the thread of the needle (eye of snow) had its loom on an indifferent scaffold—North or South—whose seamless fire was a *different* shadow, cloth over the Pole.

Yurokon spied that cloth—East, West—as it sailed on high beneath and above sister and uncle. Sailed on high, composite bird, flower, tailed beast; sailed in the spiral of the winds as he tugged gently, pulling in, paying out his twine with masterly skill. He was the child of legend and the lord of creation and his paper or map, kite or globe, was a magical witness of curious survival, the terrifying innocent play of a timeless element in all places and things. In all its manifestations it seemed to Yurokon to spell relief at the summit of his need.

His small sister, running before him, began to sing to the kite with joy.

"Eastertide again", Father Gabriel said to himself, "annunciation of music."